COMPUTER GAME ADDICT

VIRTUAL UNREALITY

Terrance Dicks

Illustrated by Laura Beaumont

ORCHARD BOOKS

ORCHARD BOOKS
96 Leonard Street, London EC2A 4RH
Orchard Books Australia
14 Mars Road, Lane Cove, NSW 2066
ISBN 1 86039 335 7 (paperback)
First published in Great Britain by Piccadilly Press Ltd 1995
First paperback publication 1997
Text © Terrance Dicks 1995
Illustrations © Laura Beaumont 1995
The right of Terrance Dicks to be identified as the author of
this work and Laura Beaumont as the illustrator has been
asserted by them in accordance with the Copyright, Designs
and Patents Act, 1988.
A CIP catalogue record for this book is available from the
British Library.
Printed in Great Britain by
The Guernsey Press Co Ltd, Vale, Guernsey, Channel Islands.

Chapter One

BRAINSTORM

Zak hunched over the controls of his Starfighter, eyes fixed on the screen of his space radar. As the photon torpedo streaked towards him he flipped the Starfighter expertly to one side. The missile streaked past, missing him by millimetres.

A second missile zoomed towards him, then a third. Zak dodged them both with the same expert skill. Then he was through, safely inside the little spaceport's defence system. He zoomed over the missile silos and landed the Starfighter right outside the big dome that was the spaceport's only building.

Zak opened the exit ramp and slid out. As he hit the ground, he was surrounded by a group of ragged, fierce-looking men, all clutching blasters and laser-rifles. Smugglers and space-pirates, the lot of them, he thought. Devil's Star was a refuge for all the scum of the galaxy.

Suddenly Zak's blaster was in his hand.

'I'm here on official business,' he said. 'Don't interfere and you won't get hurt. I'll blast anyone who gets in my way.'

Zak was badly outnumbered, and for a moment it looked as if the gang would attack him.

Then someone muttered, 'He means it. That's Captain Zak of the Space Patrol.'

The crowd fell back, and Zak strode into the spaceport.

The spaceport dome was a combination of living quarters, bar and store-room. Around the bar at the far end, a mixed crowd of humanoids and aliens, all equally villainous-looking, were shouting and arguing, knocking back weird-looking drinks.

The noise died away as Zak marched into the room.

'S-s-space Patrol!' hissed a snake-headed alien.

'Exterminate him!' grated a metal, pepper-pot-like creature.

Zak ignored them. Scanning the crowd, he fixed on a massive alien with fierce red-eyes and a wolf-like face.

'Kazor, I'm arresting you for murder.'

'You're mad,' snarled Kazor. 'Do you think you can just come in here and arrest me in the middle of all my gang?'

'You're wanted by the Space Patrol,' said Zak. 'Dead or alive. Your choice!'

Kazor stood there as if he was frozen.

'Well?' snapped Zap. 'Which is it to be?'

When Kazor still didn't speak Zak drew his blaster.

'All right, Kazor, put up your hands. You're coming with me.'

At last Kazor spoke, in a strangely high-pitched voice.

'For heavens sake, Zacharia, what do you think you're doing? Go back to your place, or I shall send you to the Head.'

Suddenly Kazor began to fade. Zak blinked and his surroundings disappeared. To his horror, he found himself not in a spaceport, but in his classroom at school.

He wasn't confronting the notorious Kazor the Killer, but the even more notorious Miss Tibbets, the school's dreaded maths teacher.

He was covering her, not with a blaster, but with a wooden ruler. Instead of a bar full of sinister aliens, he was surrounded by his astonished and amused classmates.

Zak went scarlet with embarrassment.

'Sorry, Miss,' he muttered and scuttled back to his place.

'Now that Zak has returned to his senses,' said Miss Tibbets acidly, 'perhaps we can get on with the lesson.'

Luckily, the bell went soon after that. People gave Zak some very funny looks as he left the classroom. In the playground his two best friends, tall thin Sy and round, bouncy Tom, gathered around him.

'What on Earth did you think you were doing?' asked Sy.

'First week of the new term, and already you're in trouble with Tibby the Terror!' said Tom.

'I am?' said Zak. 'What did I do?'

Sy stared at him. 'You don't remember?'

'It's a bit blurred...'

'She'd just given us this fiendish maths problem to solve,' said Tom. 'You remember that?'

'Sort of.'

'Well, I looked at you to see how you were getting on, and you weren't even trying – just staring into space.'

'That's right,' said Sy. 'Suddenly you got

up and started stalking down the aisle towards Miss Tibbets.

'All mean and slitty-eyed,' said Tom. 'Then you told her she was wanted by the Space Patrol – dead or alive!'

Sy grinned. 'Never seen anyone look so amazed!'

'She wasn't as amazed as I was when I came to and realised what I was doing,' said Zak.

'But what happened?' asked Tom. 'Were you day-dreaming? Having hallucinations?'

Sy gave him a suspicious look. 'Have you been over-doing the computer games again?'

Zak was an acknowledged computer game champion. For a time he'd been in danger of getting a bit obsessive, but some very strange adventures in cyberspace had led him to broaden his interests. He was still a bit of an addict, but he reckoned he had it well under control. Or at least, he thought he had. Now it looked as if something was controlling him!

'I've hardly played at all recently,' he said, answering Sy's question. 'We got satellite telly a few days ago, and I've spent most of my time watching that.'

Zak rubbed his eyes, wondering if the school playground was suddenly going to turn into an alien planet or the urban jungle.

'Do me a favour you two,' he said. 'Just keep an eye on me in class will you? If I have any more funny turns, sit on me quick.'

'Don't worry,' said Sy consolingly.

'Probably just a sudden freak-out – a sort of brainstorm.'

'Don't suppose it'll happen again,' said Tom.

Zak wasn't so sure. He had a nasty feeling that something very strange was going on.

When he got home after school he discovered he was right.

Waving goodbye to Sy and Tom, Zak turned off into his own street. He was still feeling worried by what had happened in class.

He'd had similar experiences before, but always in cyberspace. When they ended he found himself back in front of his own computer-screen, not making a total idiot of himself in public. This latest illusion was all mixed up with real life – a sort of virtual unreality...

'Well, at least it's Friday,' thought Zak. 'Maybe whatever it is will wear off over the weekend.'

When he reached his house he saw Mr Morris, their next door neighbour, standing outside.

Neighbourly relations with Mr Morris had always been a bit tricky. He and Zak's dad tended to quarrel about the use of the parking space between their houses. That had died down a bit recently, thanks to some peacemaking efforts by Zak.

But there'd just been a fresh outbreak of hostilities when old Morris had yelled at Zak and his friends, just for playing their radio on the local common. He said it disturbed the birds.

Zak wondered if Mr Morris was waiting to deliver another telling-off. 'Grumpy old twit,' he muttered. 'Just because he hates music. I bet the birds enjoyed it.'

As he got closer, Zak saw that there was something very strange-looking about Mr Morris. He'd got one of the long canes he used in the garden stuck in his belt and another one in his hand. What's more, he was wearing one of his wife's hats, the one with a big feather in.

When he saw Zak he swept it off and made a low bow, as they do in costume dramas on the television. 'Good day, sir, you are just in time for our meeting.'

Zak stared at him in astonishment. 'Sorry?'

'Our little affair of honour,' said Mr Morris grandly. 'Your weapon, sir!' With a flourish, he handed Zak the raspberry cane. He stepped back, drew his own cane from his belt and came on guard. 'Have at you, sir!'

He lunged at Zak, who brought up his own cane in defence.

'Oi!' yelled Zak. 'Pack it up!'

'Too late to apologise now, sir,' sneered Mr Morris. 'You have insulted the King's musketeers. For that, you die!'

He lunged at Zak with his cane.

Chapter Two

BREAKDOWN

Luckily, Zak had appeared last term in the school production of *Hamlet*. The play ends in a big duel scene and Zak had done quite a bit of fencing in rehearsal.

He parried Mr Morris's thrust, and lunged back himself.

For the next few minutes they fought a fierce duel up and down Mr Morris's front garden watched by a few fascinated passers-by.

Mr Morris fought with grim determination, cutting and thrusting and leaping on and off the low garden wall like an over-weight Errol Flynn.

It was funny in a way, but somehow it was scary as well. There was a mad gleam in Mr Morris's eye, and Zak felt that the old codger really wanted to kill him. Zak wasn't sure how much damage old Morris could do with a raspberry cane, but he didn't want to find out.

Fortunately for Zak, he was young and thin and fit. Mr Morris wasn't any of those things and he soon started puffing. The fury of his attack slowed down, he lowered his guard and Zak lunged. The point of his cane

took Mr Morris right on the belly-button. There was a sharp cracking sound and Mr Morris yelled, 'Oof!'

Zak found himself holding about a foot of raspberry cane, the rest apparently disappearing into Mr Morris's round belly.

For one ghastly moment, Zak thought the cane had gone right through him. Then he realised that it had broken off short.

Dropping his cane and clutching his tummy, Mr Morris keeled over backwards into his own flower-bed.

Zak's big brother, Sam, and his brainy little sister, Sarah, came running out of the house.

'What's going on?' asked Sam. 'I looked out of the window and saw you and old Morris having a right old ding-dong.'

'Don't ask me,' gasped Zak. 'He set about me so I had to fight back. I thought I'd killed him.'

'Stand back, I'm a first aid expert,' said Sarah bossily. (Sarah was an expert in everything.) She knelt beside Mr Morris, examined him and took his pulse.

Mr Morris opened his eyes and raised his head.

'Milady!' he gasped. 'Tell the King I died bravely...'

His eyes closed and his head fell back.

Sarah stood up. 'He's perfectly all right physically. He seems to be suffering from aggravated dementia combined with some kind of systematic paranoid delusion.'

'You mean he's gone potty!' said Sam.

Zak's mother came out of the house. 'What on earth's going on?' She looked at the still figure in the flower-bed.

'Mr Morris! What are you doing down there?'

Strangely enough, the sharp tone seemed to work. Mr Morris opened his eyes and scrambled to his feet. He looked at the stub of raspberry cane in Zak's hand. 'You've broken it,' he said accusingly. 'I'll thank you not to play about with my property, young man!' Realising that he was still wearing his wife's hat, he snatched it from his head, muttering, 'Keeps the sun off!'

He marched back into his own house, slamming the door behind him.

They told Zak's father about it when he got home from work.

'Doesn't surprise me a bit,' he said. 'I always thought old Morris was a few sandwiches short of a picnic. It's a funny coincidence, all the same.'

'What is?' asked Zak.

His father picked up the local paper. 'Quite a lot of weird things seem to have been going on round here recently. A respectable old teacher at the Technical College was arrested for dressing up in a black cloak and trying to bite a strange young lady on the neck. The Mayor stood up in a council meeting and announced he was really an alien from the planet Tharg, come to take over the world.'

Sam grabbed the paper from his father and studied it. 'And the local vicar started tap dancing down the aisle in church!'

'Surely that's just the usual newspaper rubbish?' said Zak's mother.

Zak shook his head. 'So many stories, all in the same area and all happening more or less at once?'

'Could be a sort of epidemic,' said Sarah. 'Something very similar happened in the middle ages. Some wheat rotted and produced a kind of natural LSD. Peasants all over the area went completely demented.'

'They've tightened up food standards since then,' said Zak. 'I take it the poor old peasants just went generally potty?'

Sarah nodded. 'Lots of singing and dancing and screaming and raving and rolling around on the ground.'

Sam grinned. 'Sounds just like your average pop concert!'

'There you are then,' said Zak. 'They didn't start imagining they were people out of films and books.'

'They couldn't really,' Sarah pointed out. 'Films weren't invented then. There weren't many books about either.'

'You know what I mean,' said Zak. 'There's some kind of pattern to all this – and I don't like it a bit.'

Zak was still worried when he got up next morning. To his mother's astonishment, he skipped breakfast and went out for his usual Saturday morning wander around town. Somehow he didn't want to be with his family or his friends. He wanted to think...

As he was drifting down the high street, hunger struck. He was passing the post office and decided to call in for a snack.

The post office was the usual combination of post office and newsagent. There was a counter on the left as you went in, a big glass-topped freezer compartment in the middle, and the post office bit was behind a metal grille at the far end.

Zak was peering into the freezer trying to decide between a Chunky Chokkywonder and a Raspberry Rapture when he heard a low, guttural voice behind him.

'Okay, sister, this is a stick-up. Hand over the cash and nobody gets hurt!'

Zak whirled round. There was nobody at the post office counter but a little old lady with a bag of shopping.

He was wondering if he'd imagined it when the same voice said, 'Gimme the dough or I'll drill you full of holes!'

Surprisingly, the voice was coming from the little old lady. Even more surprisingly, she was holding up the astonished post office lady, with a banana!

Zak knew who the little old lady was. Her name was Miss Perry and she lived in his street. She was a retired schoolteacher and she owned about six cats.

Zak felt he had to do something. He stepped forward.

'Hello, Miss Perry, how are all the cats?'

She swung round, covering him with her banana. 'Stay outta this kid, unless you wanna get plugged!'

Like the business with old Morris, it was funny and scary at the same time. There was exactly the same mad gleam in the old lady's eye, and it was weird hearing the tough gangster talk coming from her lips.

Zak remembered his mother speaking sharply to Mr Morris.

He raised his voice. 'Come to get your pension have you, Miss Perry?' he shouted. 'Don't spend it all on cat food!'

Miss Perry blinked and rubbed her eyes. 'Oh, hello, Zak. Yes, quite a lot goes on the cats, but I don't grudge a penny of it. I simply couldn't manage without them.'

She put the banana back in her shopping bag, produced her pension book, collected her money and tottered off.

'Poor old dear's losing her marbles,' said the post office lady. 'Must be her age.'

Zak nodded, but he didn't say anything. Miss Perry might be old, he thought, but she was still very bright. He chose the Raspberry Rapture, paid for it at the counter and went out.

Still thinking things over, Zak called in at the Video Hut on his way home, just to see what was new in the video game world. Mr Martindale, the owner, was a grumpy old soul who hated kids and video games alike, but he had the best stock for miles around. His shop was a regular hang-out for Zak and his friends.

Zak stood looking at the games in the shop window while he finished his ice-cream. There was a notice on the door 'NO FOOD OR DRINK IN SHOP' and Mr Martindale was very strict about it.

Zak licked his fingers and dropped the wrapping-paper into a bin.

As he went inside he heard a hoarse voice roar, 'Give us a kiss then, me fine buxom wench!'

An angry female voice shrieked, 'I shall do no such thing. You ought to be ashamed of yourself, Mr Martindale!'

A very large and very angry lady swept out of the shop nearly knocking Zak over. Mr

Martindale's shop was lined with working TV sets, all showing the latest video games. But today Zak was too astonished to look at any of them. All his attention was taken up by Mr Martindale himself.

Mr Martindale had a red scarf bound around his head and an inflatable rubber parrot on one shoulder. He had the shop broom tucked upside down under one arm like a crutch, and one leg was tucked up behind him.

He hopped up to Zak, moving with surprising speed. 'Jim lad!' he cried. "'Tis young Jim Hawkins, aha! Welcome aboard, lad! Time we was setting sail for Treasure Island. Aha!' He flung an arm round Zak's neck, nearly throttling him, rolling his eyes madly. 'Don't 'e betray old Long John Silver, lad, or I'll slit your gizzard with this!'

He waved something shining under Zak's nose. Zak saw with some relief that it was a table-spoon – but he'd had enough all the same.

Mr Martindale looked even madder than the old lady in the post office, and a lot more dangerous. Wriggling free, Zak turned and fled from the shop.

As he shot through the door and down the street he could hear Mr Martindale singing hoarsely:

'Sixteen men on a dead man's chest. Yo ho ho, and a bottle of rum!

Drink and the devil have done for the rest...'

'That's it!' thought Zak. 'I've got to find out what's going on.' He hurried off to the Arches to look for the Boffin.

Chapter Three

CRACK-UP

The Arches was a rather sleazy area of scruffy little shops around the old station. It took its name from the arches under the old disused railway bridge. They'd been fitted with doors at each end and rented out to little firms, mostly in the dodgy end of the car and electronic business.

The Boffin's establishment, Ultimate Electronics, was sandwiched between Ernie's Exhaust Pipes and Rod's Reconditioned Tyres – when it was there at all. Sometimes it simply disappeared and Rod and Ernie suddenly became next door neighbours again.

This was because the Boffin's shop, like the Boffin himself, really existed only in cyberspace.

The shop was there this time – somehow Zak had known that it would be. The Boffin was always there when you needed him.

Zak opened the door and went inside. The shop was like a sort of hi-tech time tunnel, lined with electronic equipment. As you came in you saw heavy old-fashioned stuff with massive valves and accumulators. Things got steadily more modern as you moved along. At the far end, surrounded by ultra-modern equipment, a tall, thin figure with a high, bald forehead, a neat pointed beard and blazing blue eyes was perched on a stool, watching an old black and white film on television.

He rose to his feet as Zak entered the shop.

'There you are, Zacharia,' said the Boffin. 'I've been expecting you. There's an evil plan afoot, and only you can prevent it!'

Zak came into the shop, giving the Boffin a suspicious look. 'Oh yes? Why me?'

'Because you're the champion,' said the Boffin, switching off the television set and sitting down again. 'You mastered the Ultimate

Game. You're the only one who can defeat the Virus!'

Zak had a funny sort of relationship with the Boffin. He liked and admired him, and in a way they were even friends. But he could never forget that the Boffin wasn't really human. He was a creature from cyberspace, the new dimension created by computers, computer games, and the internet. Cyberspace was growing so fast that it had developed life-forms of its own.

Some, like the Boffin, were benevolent. Others were evil, jealous of the human world, eager to control or even destroy it. The Virus was one of the evil ones. Zak had already tangled with him once before. He wasn't keen to do it again.

'You're sure it's the Virus?'

'Who else? Since you defeated him, he's been laying low, but I've picked up rumours that he's come up with another evil scheme. The trouble is, I can't find out what it is. But some very strange things have been happening.'

'I know,' said Zak. 'Some of them have been happening to me.'

He told the Boffin what had happened to

him in class, and of the strange behaviour of Mr Morris, Miss Perry and Mr Martindale.

The Boffin nodded. 'Things like that have been going on all around here.'

'It's pretty feeble for an evil plan, isn't it?' said Zak. 'Getting a few people to act silly? What does it matter if someone fights a duel with a raspberry cane, or holds up a post office with a banana. All very embarrassing, but no real harm done.'

'What about the people with really important jobs?' asked the Boffin. 'Suppose a train driver gets one of these delusions? Suppose it spreads, and the man in charge of the country's defence system starts zapping passing planes with his missiles?'

'That's pretty unlikely, isn't it?'

'Is it? I think some real disaster is bound to happen – it's only a matter of time.'

'What beats me is how the Virus is doing it,' said Zak. 'He was using computer games last time. I suppose Mr Martindale must see a few games, but I bet he doesn't play them for pleasure. And I can't see old Morris or Miss Perry playing games at all. I hadn't played for ages myself when I had my funny turn.'

'The Virus has discovered an entirely new method of attack,' said the Boffin solemnly. 'You must go into cyberspace, Zacharia, and hunt him down!'

'I shall do no such thing,' said Zak. 'I've had some very nasty experiences in cyberspace, remember. And that's where the Virus is most powerful.'

'The Virus knows you're his enemy. If you don't go after him, he'll come after you.'

'Let him try,' said Zak. 'If I stay away from computers and computer games for a while he can't touch me...'

Suddenly he realised that the Boffin wasn't listening. Instead, he was glaring angrily at Zak with fierce blue eyes.

'So, Ming the Merciless, you dare to attack me, here in my laboratory? Well, I, Professor Zarkoff, defy you!'

'Hang on a minute,' said Zak.

'I have invented the Zarkoff Disintegrator Cannon,' roared the Boffin. 'Prepare to die, Ming!'

The Boffin stooped down and came up with a massive futuristic-looking rifle. He fired, Zak ducked, and a shelf-full of electronic equipment above his head disintegrated in a shower of broken glass.

Feeling that this was a bad time to discuss things, Zak turned and ran, zig-zagging frantically down the long narrow shop as he made for the door.

All around him electronic equipment blew up in a shower of sparks as the Boffin blazed away. Zak reached the door at last, flung it open and leaped outside, slamming the door behind him.

He ran off down the cobbled alleyway, hoping that the Boffin wouldn't follow. Halfway down the alleyway, he glanced over his shoulder, and saw that Ernie's Exhaust Pipes and Rod's Reconditioned Tyres were next door neighbours again. The Boffin and his shop had vanished into cyberspace.

Zak made his way home, trying to make sense of what had happened. Why should the Boffin turn against him? Had it been the real Boffin at all? Was it the Virus in disguise? Somehow Zak couldn't believe it. That had been the Boffin all right, and he had been in the grip of an illusion. Whatever the Virus's new attack method, the Boffin was as vulnerable to it as anyone else. But what was it? How did it work?

Zak was quiet and thoughtful that evening, so much so that his mother was sure he was sickening for something. She was certain of it when he said he felt like an early night. Zak was a night owl – getting him to go to bed at all was usually a major battle.

The trouble was that once in bed Zak was too worked up and worried to sleep. He lay awake for ages, wondering what to do.

In the old days he'd sometimes played computer games late into the night. Zak looked at his computer and shook his head determinedly. That would make things easy for the Virus. Computer games were a gateway into cyberspace, and gates worked both ways.

Despairing of sleep, Zak got up to watch

some television. It was very late now, and everyone else was in bed. He crept into the sitting room and put on the television with the sound turned low.

Soon he was curled up on the sofa, engaged in his new past-time of channel surfing. He flicked the remote control, marvelling, at the amazing variety of channels. There was the sport, of course. At this hour it often seemed to be covering beach volleyball, wind-surfing or heavy truck racing.

There were shopping channels with lovely ladies selling you weird earrings, or madly excited men in tights flogging exercise systems that turned you into another Big Arnie in no time.

There was a batch of channels where everything was dubbed into German or Spanish, so you got old favourites like Perry Mason or Marshal Dillon rattling away in some foreign tongue.

Eventually Zak decided to watch a movie – not one of the nearly-new or made-for-TV ones, but one of the oldies. Hadn't he found an old movie channel the other night?

Zak surfed through the outer reaches of the channels, skipping over Indian epics with singing and dancing, Chinese cookery lessons, and Starsky and Hutch in Dutch.

At last he ended up on a channel called VTV. At the moment it was just playing music and displaying a list of film titles.

Before Zak could read it, the list vanished, to be replaced by a handsome presenter in full evening dress, complete with top hat and black cloak. The presenter seemed oddly familiar.

'Good evening, ladies and gentlemen,' he

purred in a smooth, velvety voice. 'Welcome to the wonderful world of VTV. We have a wonderful assortment of golden oldies tonight – films so real that you'll think they are actually happening to you. Films that will stay in your mind long after you've switched off, popping up when you least expect them.'

He laughed. It was a curiously sinister laugh.

'But first I have to announce a change of programme. We were going to start the evening's viewing with 'Space Wars'. But Zak's already seen that, haven't you, Zak?'

Zak blinked. Was the television really talking to him? He felt that he was in an odd, half-hypnotised state, as if he was dreaming.

'So since Zak's one of our favourite viewers, we're going to put on a special creature feature instead – "Monsters of the Lost Plateau".'

Suddenly the presenter changed. The handsome features dissolved, giving way to a long thin face with glossy black hair, and a little pointed beard.

'Welcome to Virus Television, Zak!' snarled the Virus.

Two incredibly long, thin arms reached out of the set, snatched Zak off the sofa, and dragged him through the screen.

Zak found himself on a rocky desert plain. He heard a shattering roar from behind him and whirled around. Peering at him from behind a jagged rock was the nastiest-looking monster he had ever seen. Somewhere between a dinosaur and a dragon it had great glowing eyes, massive horns, long, pointed fangs and a row of spikes along its back. The monster roared again, and set off towards Zak like an express train.

Zak turned and fled. Behind him he could hear the thundering feet of the monster as it pounded across the plain. It was getting closer. Suddenly Zak's foot twisted and he fell. Looking up, he saw the monster's head swooping down towards him...

Chapter Four

VIRUS TV

All at once the rocky plain and the slavering monster vanished. Zak found himself back on the sofa in the sitting room watching television – only it wasn't the real sitting room. It was an immense shadowy chamber in which a tiny Zak cowered in a huge sofa in front of an enormous television set. And there on screen, immaculate in evening dress and swirling black cloak was the presenter – the Virus!

'Not enjoying our creature feature, Zak?' purred the Virus.

'Not much,' said Zak. 'I didn't think much

of my part.'

'What a pity!' said the Virus. 'Still we must keep our best customer happy. How about another look at "Space Wars"?'

Suddenly Zak was back in the spaceport bar on Devil's Star, confronting a tall, handsome man in a white space suit.

'You're wanted by the Space Patrol, Kazor,' said the heroic figure. 'Dead or alive. Your choice.'

With sudden dread, Zak realised that this time he wasn't the hero. This time he was Kazor the Killer, the space outlaw who'd made the mistake of defying Captain Zak of the Space Patrol.

Personally, Zak would have been only too glad to surrender, but his hands seemed to have other ideas. He found himself grabbing for his blaster. The Captain's blaster was drawn and aimed before Zak's weapon cleared the holster. The blaster roared...

...and Zak was back on his sofa in that nightmare sitting room.

'Lost our taste for Space Opera?' sneered the Virus. 'What about a good old horror movie?'

Wearing strange old-fashioned clothes, Zak was climbing a narrow stone staircase. He was following a squat ugly figure who was lighting his way with a candlestick.

At the top of the stairway was a metal-studded wooden door. The door swung open with a sinister groaning sound.

The servant stood aside. 'The Count will receive you now, sir.'

Zak went through the door and found himself in an impressive dining room. Candles burned in silver candlesticks on a long mahogany dining table. A tall dark-haired man in a long black cloak stood by a blazing fire.

Trapped in the movie, Zak heard himself speaking his lines. 'I must apologise for disturbing you at this late hour. My carriage broke an axle...'

'My dear sir, don't apologise,' said the tall man. 'You are most welcome, I assure you. We get very few midnight visitors here at Castle Dracula!'

The tall man smiled evilly, revealing long sharp teeth. He glided towards Zak, who was frozen to the spot with fear.

Eyes red and fangs gleaming, the vampire sprang...

...and Zak found himself back in the sitting room.

'Not too happy with horror either, Zak?' hissed the Virus.

Zak did his best not to sound frightened. 'I forgot my garlic and my sharpened stake,' he

croaked. 'Besides, vampire's victim is a rotten part. Can't I be the hero?'

'With the greatest of pleasure,' said the Virus smoothly. 'How about captain of a starship?'

As the sitting room faded away Zak heard the Virus say, 'But I'm afraid things may be looking a bit tricky...'

Zak was standing on the bridge of a huge starship – somehow it all looked very familiar. He was surrounded by a little group of people all looking anxiously at him.

There was an attractive dark-skinned lady, an oriental-looking man, and a tall officer with strangely pointed ears.

'Allow me to summarise our position, Captain,' said the tall officer. 'Our engines are totally crippled, our energy shields useless, and we are entirely surrounded by an enemy fleet who are determined to destroy us. What are your orders?'

Zak looked around the circle of hopeful faces. They were all relying on him to come up, yet again, with the brilliant idea that would save the situation.

The only trouble was, he couldn't think of anything.

'Captain?' said the tall officer urgently. 'What can we do?'

'Er – carry on!' said Zak.

The bridge exploded in flame, Zak flew through the air...

...and landed back on the huge sofa.

'Not really up to being a Starfleet captain, are you?' sneered the Virus.

'Not in a totally impossible situation like that,' said Zak indignantly. 'If you gave me a chance...'

'All right,' said the Virus. 'How about a nice fair fight?'

Zak was standing in the centre of an arena – a huge rocky bowl surrounded with a number of gates.

A terrifying figure strode out of the gate opposite him. The creature was ten feet tall with a mass of bushy hair and six muscular arms, all whirling about aiming killer karate chops.

Another figure appeared in the gate to his left. This one was a Samurai warrior with an immensely long curved sword in each hand. It stalked towards Zak, the blades whirling in gleaming circles of steel.

From a third and fourth gate appeared a fire-breathing dragon and a giant robot. With threatening screams, howls and roars they all rushed towards Zak.

This time Zak did manage to think of something.

As the circle of enemies came closer, Zak leaped high into the air, and his monstrous enemies all crashed into each other. Below him he saw the six-armed being tackle the Samurai and the dragon blasting the robot. Zak began falling, down, down, down...

...and landed back on his sofa, with the Virus sneering at him from the screen.

'That wasn't a fair fight!' protested Zak when he got his breath back. 'And that was no movie, it was a beat-'em-up computer game!'

'Not a bit of it,' said the Virus smoothly. 'It was a movie based on a beat-'em-up. Everything's changing so fast, Zak. You must try to keep up. These days there are games based on movies, movies based on games... There are even games with interactive movies built in. But it all happens in cyberspace, and that means you can control it – and use it to attack your human world!'

The Virus stroked his pointed beard. 'Well, it's nearly close-down time, Zak. I think we'll end on the creature feature after all. The scene where the monster eats the explorer is a classic, you know – even though it was criticised for excessive violence. Buckets of blood all over the place – your blood! Enjoy the movie, Zak. It's the last one you'll ever see.'

The Virus gave a mocking peal of maniacal laughter...

...and Zak was back on the rocky plain, with the monster's head plunging down. He rolled to one side and the teeth snapped shut, missing him by inches.

Zak scrambled to his feet and ran, the monster pounding after him. He knew that this time the danger was real.

Up to now, the Virus had just been playing with him, snatching him away from danger in the nick of time. Of course, the monster wasn't real, except in cyberspace. But although Zak's body was actually safe at home, his mind, his whole personality, were in cyberspace – with the monster.

If it caught him and chomped him up, his real body might die from psychic shock. Either that, or he'd become a mindless vegetable. He'd be found in front of the television by his parents next morning like one of those newspaper stories – an awful example of the effects of too much TV and too many computer games.

Zak dodged behind a little rock and the monster snapped at him and got the rock instead. It was delayed for a second, spitting out chunks of rock and Zak gained a bit of a lead.

His mind, like his feet, was working at double speed. Zak knew that to some extent, he could control events in cyberspace. The trouble was that everything was moving too fast for him to think – no doubt the Virus was keeping things that way on purpose.

Suddenly a strange idea struck him. Perhaps he could only save himself in some way that made sense inside the movie.

Running and dodging frantically at the same time, Zak tried to remember all the old late-night monster movies he'd ever seen.

What happened when the hero was in a spot like this? How did the scriptwriter get him out of it? What could logically turn up on the Lost Plateau to stop a monster? Of course...

Zak struggled to remember a recent visit to the Natural History Museum.

With a shattering scream, another monster appeared from behind one of the big rocks ahead. It was short and stubby and it was entirely covered in knobbles and spikes. It looked no match for the first monster, but it roared a challenge all the same.

When it saw the second monster, the first monster lost interest in Zak. Whirling round, it rushed towards this new enemy like an express train.

At this point, monster number two revealed its secret weapon. It had an immensely long tail with a spiked ball on the end of it. When the first monster charged, it whirled the tail through the air and struck its attacker the most tremendous clump on the head. Monster number one staggered back dazed, shook its head and renewed the attack.

All well and good, thought Zak, as he watched the two great creatures roar and slash at each other. But eventually one of the monsters was bound to win, and the winner might well feel like a little snack.

If he ran they might leave off fighting to chase him. Even if they didn't, he could still die in the desert.

So how could he get out of trouble this time?

Chapter Five

REWRITE

Zak thought hard. At this point the hero, if he survived, usually had to be rescued by his trusty sidekick.

Zak peered at the horizon and was pleased to see a little cloud of dust in the distance. It drew nearer and turned into a big Land Rover, driven by a tall, thin figure in baggy shorts and a huge solar topee.

It was the Boffin.

'Get in Zacharia,' he shouted, as the Land Rover roared up.

Zak jumped in and the Boffin drove away at top speed. Gradually the roars of the battling monsters died away.

'What's going on?' asked the Boffin as they bounced across the desert. 'I was in my shop worrying about you and I suddenly found myself here.'

'I brought you here,' explained Zak. 'You're my faithful sidekick come to drive me back to camp.'

Sure enough, a little cluster of tents appeared ahead of them. They parked the jeep and white-robed servants ran out to look after them. Soon Zak and the Boffin were sitting in canvas chairs outside the main tent with long cool drinks in their hands.

The camp was at the edge of a massive plateau with steep walls falling away to reveal thick jungle far below.

Zak studied the spectacular view. 'We must be in one of those Lost World movies,' he said. 'You're the mad professor who always believed there was a plateau full of prehistoric monsters hidden somewhere in the heart of Africa. I'm the heroic hunter you persuaded to guide you there. I wouldn't be surprised if you had a beautiful daughter who insisted on coming on the expedition.'

'Never mind her,' said the Boffin severely. 'Things are quite complicated enough already. We're in one of the Virus's traps. I realised what must be happening after that business in my shop. I'd been watching that wretched VTV of his and he used it to turn me against you. I do apologise, Zacharia.'

'Not your fault,' said Zak. 'The same thing happened to me and to those people I met.

Movies on satellite exist in cyberspace too. The Virus has found a way to use them to affect people's minds.'

'So how do we get out?' asked the Boffin. 'If it's the Virus's movie, that means he's in control.'

'Not entirely,' said Zak. 'We can affect things too. That's how I escaped, and brought you here.'

'The Virus is more in control,' insisted the Boffin. 'He set the whole thing up just to trap you. He's bound to attack again soon.'

Zak pointed back the way they'd come. 'You're right – look!'

A wall of dust was moving across the desert. As the wall came nearer it turned into a line of monsters. There were savage creatures of every shape and size, snakes, gorillas and dinosaurs included. Stalking ahead of them, immaculate in full evening dress, was the Virus.

Soon the little camp was entirely surrounded by a semi-circle of monsters – wall to wall claws and fangs.

'A mass attack of monsters!' said Zak almost admiringly.

'It's the final sequence, Zak,' called the Virus. 'Final for you, anyway. My little pets will advance, eat you, or drive you back and back, until you fall to your deaths over the edge of the plateau.'

Slowly the monsters advanced. Zak and the Boffin backed away. The monsters came on, tramping over the tents, until Zak and the Boffin were at the very edge of the plateau with a sheer drop behind them.

'Think, Zacharia!' urged the Boffin. 'How do we get out of this?'

'I don't know,' confessed Zak. 'The trouble is movies don't change. They're exactly the same every time you see them.'

Suddenly Zak remembered what the Virus had said earlier.

'There are games based on movies, movies based on games... There are even games with interactive movies built in.'

'Yes they do!' shouted Zak. 'These days movies do change! That's it!'

He concentrated with all his might...

... and suddenly Zak and the Boffin were in an ultra-modern control room. It was lined with screens and crammed with complicated equipment. On the biggest screen, right in front of them, they saw themselves, retreating before the line of monsters, getting nearer and nearer to the cliff edge...

Zak rushed to the main console and adjusted controls. The picture froze and then went into reverse.

Marching backwards across the screen, behind his retreating monsters, the Virus looked up. 'Hey, stop this. It's not fair!'

'Shut up you,' said Zak. 'You're in my movie now!'

He began working frantically at the controls.

Somehow his fingers knew what to do.

'What's going on, Zacharia?' asked the baffled Boffin. 'What, in cyberspace, are you doing?'

Zak went on working. 'Something the Virus said gave me the idea. These days they're making computer games with interactive movies built in. They shoot them specially, with real actors and actresses and a budget of millions. I'm taking the Virus's

movie and building it into my computer game. That way I'm in control and he's not – I hope!'

'Will it really work, Zacharia?' asked the Boffin anxiously.

'Can you really imprison someone as powerful as the Virus in a computer game?'

'I can try,' said Zak grimly.

Suddenly the control room began spinning round and round...

...and Zak woke up in his armchair – his real armchair in his real sitting room, in front of his real television, which seemed to be showing an old episode of 'Bonanza' dubbed into Chinese.

'Must have dropped off,' muttered Zak sleepily. 'Got to give up all this late-night satellite telly.'

Then he remembered all that had happened.

Zak did a quick surf around the channels.

There was still the truck-racing and wind-surfing, the shopping channels with the love-ly ladies and the weird earrings, the muscu-lar men in tights flogging exercise systems. There were still old American TV series dubbed into German or Spanish, Indian epics, Chinese cookery lessons, and Starsky and Hutch in Dutch. But there was no sign of anything called VTV.

'Well, that's a start,' thought Zak.

He realised that there was something in his hand. It was a computer-game cartridge. On it was a hand-written label: 'Monsters of the Lost Plateau.'

Zak switched off the television, unplugged it, and went back to his room. He sat down at his computer and switched it on. He sat there for quite some time. Did the spinning, disap-pearing control-room mean that his plan had worked? Or had the Virus escaped after all?

Zak had had enough. He wanted no more monsters, no more cyberspace, just a good night's sleep.

'Got to find out if it works sometime,' he muttered. 'Best get it over with.' He loaded the game.

The opening film sequence showed three people having a conference outside a tent in the jungle. There was a handsome young hunter, who looked like a grown-up Zak, an old professor, who looked like the Boffin, and the professor's beautiful daughter, who looked like all the glamorous film-starlets you've ever seen.

Suddenly the hunter looked out of the screen in close-up. 'Glad you could join us. We're planning to rescue our friend Lord de Vere, who's disappeared on the Lost Plateau. We're trying to decide whether to go by river and risk the crocodiles, or by Umbopo country and chance the head-hunters? What do you think?'

A little on-screen menu offered Zak a choice. He chose river. After a series of exciting adventures involving white-water rapids and crocodiles, with important choices to be made at vital points, they reached the bottom of the Lost Plateau.

The professor's beautiful daughter looked out of the screen. 'Oh, I wonder how poor Lord de Vere is getting on. I do hope he survives long enough to be rescued.'

The picture changed to a desert with Lord de Vere – the Virus – still in full evening dress, being chased by a small but nasty dinosaur. He scrambled onto a rock and looked out of the screen at Zak.

'I know you're there, Zak! Get me out of here or you'll be sorry! It's not fair making me spend all day dodging monsters!'

'You did the same to me!'

'That was only my little joke!'

'Well, this is mine ,' said Zak. 'You can stay in the "Lost Plateau" game till you're too tired to get up to any more mischief. Now I'd move on if I were you. I think that dinosaur's planning another leap!'

Zak touched his joy-pad and the dinosaur sprang and missed.

The Virus gave a yell and dashed off, black cloak streaming out behind him.

'That'll teach him,' said Zak. 'Not a bad little game, that!'

He switched off the machine and went to bed.

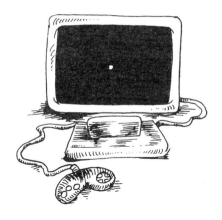

Other books in the series:

THE ULTIMATE GAME

Zacharia Jones is a real computer game addict, an expert player of every game on the market. The trouble is, he finds them all too easy.

Then Zak hears rumours about The Ultimate Game – the invention of an eccentric computer genius.

Zak finally tracks it down. But when he begins to play it, he finds himself *inside* the game – one of a troop of soldiers besieging a castle!

And playing The Ultimate Game means Zak just finishes one death-defying adventure when he's whirled into another...

Cyberspace Adventure

Everyone at school is talking about the computer crisis, and Zak finds himself going home by way of Video Gulch. There the Boffin is waiting for him with the news that The Virus in cyberspace is beginning to interfere with computer-driven operations everywhere!

Something has to be done, and fast, and someone must go into cyberspace to destroy The Virus. All Zak's computer game genius is needed to overcome the incredible dangers and defeat not only The Virus, but all the other monsters in the strange, nightmarish landscape...